Butterfly Meadow

Skipper to the Rescue

Olivia Moss

Illustrated by Sam Chaffey

SCHOLASTIC

With special thanks to Sue Mongredien

First published in the UK in 2008 by Scholastic Children's Books
An imprint of Scholastic Ltd
Euston House, 24 Eversholt Street
London, NW1 1DB, UK
Registered office: Westfield Road, Southam, Warwickshire, CV47 0RA
SCHOLASTIC and associated logos are trademarks and/or registered
trademarks of Scholastic Inc.
Series created by Working Partners Ltd.

Text copyright © Working Partners, 2008
Illustration copyright © Sam Chaffey, 2008

The moral right of the author and illustrator of this work
has been asserted by them.

Cover illustration © Sam Chaffey, 2008

ISBN 978 1 407 10657 1

Printed by
CPI Bookmarque, Croydon, CR0 4TD
Papers used by Scholastic Children's Books are made
from wood grown in sustainable forests.

1 3 5 7 9 10 8 6 4 2

www.scholastic.co.uk/zone

To Tom Powell

CONTENTS

CHAPTER ONE

New Furry Friends

It was a windy day in Butterfly Meadow. Tree branches waved as another strong breeze gusted past. Everything looked alive with movement. *Whoooooosh!* The long grasses of Butterfly Meadow swayed in the wind.

"It makes me want to fly high into the sky," Dazzle said to her friend Skipper, as the breeze tugged at her small, yellow wings.

"Me too," Skipper replied. "Let's go exploring." She fluttered with her blue wings over to Twinkle, a Peacock butterfly, and Mallow, a Cabbage White, who were balancing on nearby flowers. "We're going flying. Want to come?"

"OK," Mallow agreed, wiggling her antennae.

Twinkle looked up from admiring her colourful wings. "Sounds like fun," she said. "Let's go!"

The four friends took to the air, sailing along on the breeze. "This is so cool," Mallow cried breathlessly as the wind carried them towards the forest. "Wheeeeee!"

Dazzle was enjoying the ride too. She barely had to flap her wings as they soared over the meadow. She gazed down at the flowers below, watching their bright heads bob and dance. "Hey," Dazzle said, noticing something unusual. "What are those white things?" She pointed with her wing-tip to where three furry creatures hopped in the grass. Dazzle hadn't been out of her cocoon for long and was still making new discoveries.

Skipper peered down. "They're bunnies," she replied. "Baby rabbits. Cute, aren't they?"

Dazzle was curious. "Back in a moment," she called to her friends and swooped down towards the bunnies. As she approached, Dazzle could see that they all had long, fluffy ears and white whiskers.

Dazzle landed gently on one of the bunnies' pink noses. "Hello," she said.

The bunny laughed. "That tickles!" he said. "Say, what are you? You're not a bunny."

Dazzle smiled. "I'm a butterfly," she told him. "Am I the first butterfly you've ever seen?"

"Yes, I think you must be," the bunny said. Then he sneezed, sending Dazzle up into the air. "*Atchooo!* This is a great tickling game. Why don't you go and tickle my brother's nose, too? He loves being tickled!"

Dazzle glanced up to see that Skipper, Mallow and Twinkle were small specks, high up in the sky. "I'm sorry, I can't play right now. I'd better go catch up with my friends. I'd love to play with you another time. Bye!"

"Bye!"
all of the bunnies
chorused. Peeping back
over her wing, Dazzle
saw the bunnies all sitting
up on their hind legs
watching her go.

Dazzle raced to catch up with her friends, who had reached the forest by now. She found them near a tree.

"Dazzle," Mallow called. "Come and play – we're dodging the sycamore seeds."

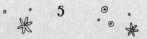

The long green sycamore seeds were falling from the tree, twisting and turning as they floated to the ground. Dazzle's friends zipped in and out of them, laughing. Skipper was particularly good at darting in between them, swerving nimbly to avoid being hit.

Dazzle joined in. "This is fun!" she cried, ducking and diving like her friends. "I love the way the seeds spin round and round. They look almost like butterflies with their wings."

"Those little wings help the seeds float away from the tree," Twinkle explained. "They'll have a better chance of growing if they don't land next to the mother tree's roots. Isn't that clever?"

Just then, a stronger gust of wind blew through the forest, and Dazzle had to dive away from the tree to avoid the shower of seeds. She gazed around, floating in the air. Where had her friends gone?

Then she heard Skipper's voice call from a beautiful black cherry tree brimming with white flowers. "Hey!" Skipper called excitedly. "Over here. Come and see what I've found!"

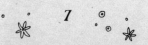

CHAPTER TWO

An Exciting Discovery

Dazzle, Mallow and Twinkle flew straight to the tree. "What is it?" Twinkle asked, perching on a branch.

"Look," Skipper said softly, pointing with a wing.

Dazzle wasn't sure what Skipper was so excited about. All she could see was a peice of dried leaf that was attached at both ends to a twig. It looked as if the leaf had been folded to make a long, thin pocket.

"A leaf?" Dazzle asked, confused.

"Not *just* a leaf," Skipper replied with

a mysterious smile.

Mallow tipped her head to one side thoughtfully. "Something to eat?" she guessed.

"A gift for me?" Twinkle wondered hopefully, twirling excitedly.

"No," said Skipper. "It's a caterpillar sleeping bag."

Twinkle and Mallow both cheered and flew loop-the-loops in mid-air.

Dazzle didn't understand why they all seemed so happy. "A caterpillar sleeping bag?" she echoed. She took a closer look. It didn't look like a cosy place to sleep, it was just a crumpled leaf.

"That's right," Skipper said. "And there's something very special inside it – a baby butterfly!"

"Oh!" Dazzle exclaimed. "That's a cocoon? Wow!" She had only seen one cocoon before – her own, and it had all been ripped apart by the time she'd emerged. Dazzle tapped gently on the dried leaf. "Hey, baby butterfly," she said softly. "Want to come out and play?"

The wind blew through the tree again, and the cocoon swung on its twig like a small brown flag.

"It doesn't

work like that," Mallow said kindly to Dazzle. "Butterflies only come out when they're ready."

Twinkle had darted into a cluster of blossoms nearby and was drinking nectar from one of the blooms. "Think of your first day as a butterfly," she said, raising her head. "No one was waiting for you to come out, were they?"

Dazzle thought back to how she'd struggled in the darkness. She could remember the way she'd burst from her cocoon into the light. The world had seemed so bright! Dazzle had been excited, but lonely and scared too. "I think I'll wait for the butterfly to come out," she announced. "I'd like to be here to welcome it."

Twinkle finished her nectar and gazed up at the sky. "I think we should head back to Butterfly Meadow," she said. "It's getting dark."

"Let's play tag first," Skipper suggested, and tapped Mallow with her wing. "Tag – you're it!" And away she flew.

While her friends chased one another around the trees, Dazzle perched near the cocoon.

"Hello," she said to it. "I wonder what sort of butterfly you'll be?"

She suddenly stopped talking and stared at the cocoon. Something was twitching inside it. Was the baby butterfly about to emerge?

CHAPTER THREE

A Storm Brews

The cocoon gave another little jiggle. Yes –
something was happening in there!

"Hey!" Dazzle called to her friends. "I
think the baby butterfly is ready to come
out."

Skipper, Mallow and Twinkle all zoomed
over. But now the cocoon wasn't doing
anything! A ladybird was walking along
the branch and stopped at the sight of the
butterflies clustered around. "What are
you all looking at?" the ladybird asked
in surprise.

"It's a cocoon," Dazzle replied. "And I thought it was about to hatch into a baby butterfly but. . ."

"Never mind. It was probably the wind making it move," Twinkle said.

Skipper looked up at the sky. "That storm's getting closer," she said.

The ladybird gazed up too. "You're right," she said. "Time for me to take cover." She scuttled away, her shiny, red wings bouncing from side to side as she ran.

Dazzle shook her head. "You know, I don't think it was the wind. I'm sure I saw it—" Then the cocoon twitched again. "There! Did you see that?"

"I did," Skipper said. "It definitely moved."

"I saw it too," Twinkle added, twirling in the air. "Oh, this is so exciting! I wonder if the new butterfly will be as pretty as me?"

The branches rattled and the whole tree swayed as the wind raced through the forest. Dazzle shivered. Dark, grey clouds were rolling across the sky, blocking the sun.

A dazzling white flash and a loud cracking sound made them all jump. Dazzle felt frightened. She had never seen anything like this before. "What's happening?" she asked.

"There's going to be a thunderstorm," Skipper told her with a nervous glance at the sky. "We need to take cover before it starts raining. If our wings get wet, we won't be able to fly home."

Dazzle's wings trembled as she and her friends sheltered under one of the larger branches of the tree. The wind whipped through the forest, making the trees groan and bend. She had enjoyed sailing on the breeze earlier but now she was worried the wind might blow her away.

Another fierce gust of wind tore through the trees, sending leaves flying from the branches. And then . . . oh no! Dazzle saw a large leaf bump into the cocoon and knock it clean away from its twig.

Dazzle and her friends watched as the cocoon sailed through the air and down to the grass. "Come on," Dazzle cried, forgetting the storm. "We have to make sure the baby butterfly is OK."

She and her friends struggled to fly down to where the cocoon had landed. It was so hard to fly into the wind. No matter how hard Dazzle batted her wings, the wind kept trying to push her back.

But just as Dazzle was starting to think it was hopeless, the wind dipped, and she and her butterfly friends landed on the grass by the cocoon. "How will the butterfly climb out safely when there's a thunderstorm?" Dazzle asked.

"We need to roll the cocoon to a place where it will be safe," Skipper decided. "Let's push it up against the tree trunk – it will be sheltered from the wind and rain there."

The four butterflies pushed hard. "Come on, team," Mallow called out as they leaned against the cocoon. But it was no good. They weren't strong enough to move it.

The ladybird they'd met earlier flew overhead. "The storm's almost here," she called out. "You'd better go some place dry."

Dazzle watched her go. There was an eerie silence in the forest now.

"We need to get the cocoon under cover before the rain starts," Skipper said. "But how?"

CHAPTER FOUR

Go Bunnies!

Dazzle suddenly had a brilliant idea!

"The bunnies might be able to help," she said.

Skipper clapped her wings together in excitement. "Good thinking! Dazzle – you and Mallow see if you can find them. Twinkle and I will stay here and guard the cocoon."

Dazzle nodded. "Don't come out until I'm back," she whispered to the cocoon.

Then she and Mallow fluttered through the gusting wind towards the meadow. She felt afraid for the baby butterfly. "Imagine coming out into the world during a storm," she said to Mallow as they flew. "It would be so scary."

"Terrifying," Mallow agreed. "I hope those bunnies can help."

"There they are," Dazzle said, spotting three fuzzy white shapes bouncing in and out of a rabbit-hole. "Let's go ask."

"It's the flutter-fly again!" yelled the smallest bunny in excitement as Dazzle

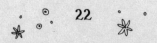

and Mallow swooped down to them.

"No, it's a flutter-by," a second bunny piped up.

"Actually, we're butterflies," Mallow said. "And we really need your help!"

She and Dazzle quickly explained what had happened.

"Of course we'll help!" the smallest bunny said.

"We like you flutter-bys," the second bunny added.

"It's butter – oh, never mind," Dazzle said. "This way – follow us!"

The two butterflies flew overhead while the three bunnies bounced after them.

"The baby is definitely ready to hatch," Skipper told Dazzle as they drew nearer the tree. "Look, you can see it vibrating inside."

Dazzle swooped down to have a look. Skipper was right! there was movement under the papery surface of the cocoon. Wow – it was so exciting that a new baby butterfly was about to be born!

"What do we do?" the smallest bunny asked.

"Well," Skipper began, "I think the best place for the cocoon to shelter would be in the hollow over there, between the roots." She pointed a wing-tip to a hole at the base of the tree. "Could you use your paws to gently nudge it there?"

"Of course!" the bunnies chorused, gathering around the cocoon.

The cocoon wriggled again.

It's almost as if the baby butterfly knows the bunnies want to help, Dazzle thought.

"Go, bunnies! Go, bunnies!" Mallow cheered, as the bunnies pushed at the cocoon with their soft paws. It bounced slowly along the ground.

"Keep going," Dazzle called out. The other creatures in the forest were tucking themselves into safe places, she noticed. Hedgehogs were curling into tight balls, birds were flying to their nests

and all the crickets had fallen silent. She couldn't help but worry. Just how bad was this thunderstorm going to be?

The bunnies had almost nudged the cocoon to the hollow when a larger rabbit hopped up. She twitched her whiskers crossly.

"There you are!" she scolded the bunnies. "I've been looking everywhere for you. Can't you feel that wind? A storm is coming. You need to get back to the burrow at once."

Dazzle flew down to explain. "They're

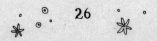

just helping us push this cocoon to shelter—" she began, but the mother rabbit wouldn't listen.

"And I need to get my babies to a safe place," she said. "Come on, all of you. Hop to it!"

"Yes, Mummy," the bunnies chorused.

"Sorry," the smallest bunny whispered to the butterflies as they hopped away. Dazzle couldn't blame them. They had to listen to their mummy. She was only trying to keep them safe.

A second flash of bright light filled the air, followed by a loud rumble.

"The storm's getting closer," Twinkle said fearfully. "The thunder came really fast after the lightning – it's nearly here!"

CHAPTER FIVE

Woof! Woof!

The butterflies heard the sound of barking and the cocoon jerked, as if the noise had made it jump. Dazzle couldn't see a dog anywhere, though. "That'll be Buster," Mallow explained, noticing her look around. "He's the sheepdog who works in the field beyond those trees."

"That's it!" Skipper cried. "Buster's good at herding sheep. I'm sure he could move one tiny cocoon to safety. I'll go ask him right away."

"Me too," Dazzle said. With a last glance

at the cocoon, she followed Skipper towards the field where a black-and-white dog was herding a flock of sheep into their shelter. Buster's ears were pricked and his tail lashed the ground; Dazzle could tell he was really concentrating.

She dived lower, darting in front of him to catch his eye, but long, shaggy hair swung in front of his eyes. "He can't see me," she called to Skipper.

"Let's both try," Skipper suggested. The two butterflies danced before the dog's face, but Buster suddenly chased after a sheep, and they had to dive out of the way. One of the sheep gazed up at Dazzle.

"He's only interested in us," it said wearily. "He won't stop until we're all safe in our shelter."

"Thanks," Dazzle said politely.

"I'll try getting closer," Skipper said. She flew to Buster's left ear, and came as close as she could. "Buster! We need your—"

But her soft wings must have tickled Buster and he flapped his ears, as if he was trying to brush away a fly. Skipper had to dodge quickly out of the way.

"*Woof! Woof!*" Buster barked so loudly at the last sheep, that Dazzle felt her wings shake.

"You take cover under the fence at the side of the field there. It's going to rain any second," Skipper said. "No use both of us getting caught in the rain."

"But. . ." Dazzle didn't want to leave her friend. "What will you do if the rain starts? Remember when Twinkle got her wings wet? She couldn't fly."

"I'll be OK," Skipper told her bravely. "I was good at dodging the sycamore seeds, wasn't I? I'll dodge the raindrops too, if I need to. Now go!"

CHAPTER SIX

Skipper Steps In

Skipper was already fluttering back towards Buster, so Dazzle flew to shelter beneath the fence. The sky was darker than ever. It was all up to Skipper now.

Skipper flew behind Buster as he herded the last sheep into the shelter. "That's it, ladies. Keep moving!" he barked. As one of the biggest sheep was trotting in, Skipper began flying in large circles above it's head. The sheep craned it's neck back to watch Skipper fly round and round. The sheep's head turned in circles as it tried to see

what Skipper would do next. *She'll get dizzy!* Dazzle thought to herself. Buster barked impatiently. "Come along!" he said to the sheep. "No stragglers here, please." But the sheep wouldn't move, even though fat drops of rain were starting to fall.

"What a beautiful butterfly!" Dazzle heard the sheep cry out – and then Buster gazed up. At last! He saw Skipper circling and shook the shaggy fur from his eyes for a better look.

"Well, I never," he said loudly.

Dazzle gave a cheer. Clever Skipper! Now she just had to persuade Buster to come and help move the cocoon. Dazzle could see that the little blue butterfly was hovering by Buster's ear and guessed that Skipper was telling the dog what had happened.

Then Buster ran towards the fence with Skipper flitting above his head.

"Yay!" Dazzle cheered, as the dog jumped through a gap in the fence.

"He's going to try and help," Skipper said, sounding relieved. "Nobody can round up animals like Buster!"

Back in the forest, heavy raindrops were pattering down. One missed Dazzle by an antenna-length and she had to keep swerving to avoid getting her wings wet.

"Take shelter under me!" Buster barked to the butterflies. "Fly under my belly – you'll be dry there."

Dazzle didn't need to be told twice. She and Skipper swooped down until they almost brushed the ground, then ducked beneath Buster's thick, shaggy fur.

"Phew," Dazzle sighed. "I don't like the rain."

"Me neither," Skipper agreed.

Lightning flashed again and the thunder boomed overhead, making both butterflies jump. Buster let out a whine of anxiety as he ran.

"We're almost there," Skipper called to him. "Head for that black cherry tree."

Buster ran through the rain to the tree, where Mallow and Twinkle were waiting. "Over here!" Dazzle heard Twinkle shout. "This way!"

Buster slowed down. Dazzle and Skipper flew out from under his belly and showed him the little cocoon lying on the ground, still wriggling. Thunder growled above them once more, and then lightning flashed. In the burst of bright light, Dazzle saw the cocoon crack – and the tip of a tiny wing poke through.

"Quickly!" she shouted. "There's no time to lose!"

CHAPTER SEVEN

A New Arrival

Buster gingerly picked up the cocoon between his jaws.

Dazzle could hardly watch as he carried it over to the tree trunk. His teeth were so sharp. What if he accidentally bit through it?

"Go, Buster!" Mallow was cheering. "Almost there!"

The rain was pouring so hard, Buster didn't see a rabbit-hole in the ground and stumbled – but he righted himself at the last moment, and took the last few steps to the tree. He gently set down the wiggling cocoon and nudged it inside the hollow. Then he lay down at the entrance so that it was sheltered from the wind. The baby butterfly was safe from the storm at last.

Dazzle, Skipper, Twinkle and Mallow all flew into the hollow too. It was cosy and dry in there, and they could hear the rain drumming outside. "Thank you, Buster!" Dazzle said in relief. They had done it.

"Oh, look!" Twinkle cried. "We were just in time."

The split in the cocoon was growing

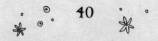

larger. A crumpled, fragile wing slowly emerged ... and another. Then the baby butterfly tentatively put out his legs.

"What's happening?" came a small voice from inside the cocoon.

"It's all right, keep going!" Dazzle called out.

Then the cocoon fell away from the tiny insect and he unfolded his wings for the first time.

Dazzle felt more excited than ever before. "Hello," she said softly. "Welcome."

The little butterfly gazed around in wonder, and opened his wings fully. Even in the gloomy darkness of the hollow, Dazzle could see that they were beautiful, shimmery blue wings with red and orange spots.

"Oh, aren't you tiny?" she said.

The baby butterfly looked at her. "Is that my name?" he asked. "Is my name Tiny?"

The other butterflies smiled. "If you like," Skipper replied. "I think Tiny is a perfect name for you."

"I'm Dazzle," Dazzle said, "and these are my friends – Skipper, Twinkle and Mallow. It's so nice to meet you at last, Tiny."

Tiny gazed around at them all. "Hi," he said shyly. "What's that noise?" he asked, peering out of the hollow past Buster, where the rain was still pelting down.

"It's a storm," Dazzle told him. "We brought you in here to keep you dry. If it wasn't for Skipper's bravery and quick thinking, you might have been stuck out there."

Tiny smiled at Skipper. "Thank you," he said. "I'm glad you helped me."

"It was no problem," Skipper replied.

Tiny stared at his wings and then at everyone else's. "Why do we all look so different?" he wondered. The question reminded Dazzle of her first moments as a butterfly. She hadn't even know what kind of creature she was at first.

"We're different types of butterfly," Twinkle explained kindly. She spread her colourful wings with a proud flourish. "My beautiful markings show that I'm a Peacock butterfly."

"I'm a Holly Blue," Skipper went on, "Mallow is a Cabbage White and Dazzle's a Pale Clouded Yellow." She peered at Tiny's

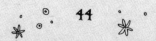

markings. "I'd say you're a Red-Spotted Purple butterfly."

"That means you're almost as gorgeous as me," Twinkle said.

Tiny gave his wings a little flap. "And will I be able to fly?" he asked.

Dazzle smiled at him. "Of course," she said, and peeked outside. The rain had stopped. "The storm's over," she told Tiny. "Do you want to try flying now?"

CHAPTER EIGHT

Flying High

"Oh yes!" Tiny cried, bouncing up and down and flapping his wings. He floated up into the air for a few seconds, looking surprised – and the other butterflies laughed.

"He's a natural," Mallow giggled. "Come on, Tiny, you're definitely ready to fly. That's all you have to do – just flap your wings."

"See if you can flutter outside," Skipper suggested. "That's it, keep flapping!"

Tiny flapped his wings energetically ... and flew straight into the side of Buster.

"Oops," Tiny said, laughing.

Buster gave a friendly *woof* and got to his feet.

"That's Buster," Dazzle said, smiling. "He's the dog who carried you to safety."

"Oh," Tiny said, wide-eyed. "Thank you, Buster."

"You're welcome," Buster replied.

"Buster!" Someone was calling to the dog.

It sounds like the friendly sheep we met earlier,
Dazzle thought.

Buster gave the butterflies a wink. "I'd better get back," he said. "Those sheep can't get along without me."

The butterflies flew out of the hollow. Now that the storm had passed, other animals were emerging from their shelters, too. Birds chirruped overhead, and the insects scuttled out. And then the bunnies hopped up, excited to meet the new baby butterfly.

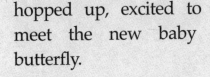

"These are bunnies," Twinkle told Tiny as he gazed up at their friendly, fluffy faces. "And they tried their hardest to keep you safe too."

"Hi," Tiny said. "Thank you. I'm really lucky to have had so much help on my first day as a butterfly." He flapped his wings and took off again. "Wheeee! Look at me!"

"Go, Tiny!" the bunnies cheered.

After a little more practise, Tiny was able to fly high into the air. The clouds had drifted away, and the sun was shining.

"Let's go back to Butterfly Meadow," Twinkle suggested. "Tiny, we can introduce you to all the other butterflies. I know you'll like it there."

Tiny did a little loop-the-loop. "I love being a butterfly!" he cried happily.

The butterflies said goodbye to the bunnies and set off for home. As they left the forest, Dazzle could see raindrops clinging to spiders' webs in the grass, and the sky was now a beautiful, clear blue.

She glanced back to make sure Tiny was all right and saw that he was keeping up beautifully, flapping his wings and beaming. "I love flying!" he called.

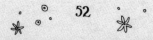

Dazzle smiled at him. *How wonderful, she thought, as she flew home. Four butterflies set out exploring today, and now five of us are flying*

back to Butterfly Meadow. Their adventures had been scary. But they'd found a new butterfly. And even better than that – they'd made a new friend.

Want to know all about the butterflies
in the meadow?

Dazzle

Pale Clouded Yellow butterfly

Likes: Dancing and making friends

Dislikes: Being left out

Twinkle

Peacock butterfly

Likes: Her beautiful wings

Dislikes: Getting wet!

Mallow

Cabbage White butterfly

Likes: Organizing parties and activities

Dislikes: Being bored

Skipper

Holly Blue butterfly

Likes: Helping others

Dislikes: Birds who try to eat her!

Read about more adventures in
Butterfly Meadow

FLUTTERY, FRIENDLY FUN

Butterfly Meadow

Dazzle's First Day

Olivia Moss

FLUTTERY, FRIENDLY FUN

Butterfly Meadow

Twinkle Dives In

Olivia Moss

FLUTTERY, FRIENDLY FUN

Butterfly Meadow

Mallow's Top Team

Olivia Moss

And coming soon

FLUTTERY, FRIENDLY FUN

Butterfly Meadow

Dazzle's Prickly Problem

Olivia Moss

FLUTTERY, FRIENDLY FUN

Butterfly Meadow

Twinkle and the Busy Bee

Olivia Moss

If you enjoyed the Butterfly Meadow series,
then look out for:

The Fairy House